Cutting-Edge STEM

Cutting-Edge
Computing with Raspberry Pi

Krystyna Poray Goddu

Lerner Publications ◆ Minneapolis

Lerner Publications Company
A division of Lerner Publishing Group, Inc.
241 First Avenue North
Minneapolis, MN 55401 USA

For reading levels and more information, look up this title at www.lernerbooks.com.

Main body text set in Adrianna Regular 14/20.
Typeface provided by Chank.

Library of Congress Cataloging-in-Publication Data

Names: Goddu, Krystyna Poray, author.
Title: Cutting-edge computing with Raspberry Pi / Krystyna Poray Goddu.
Description: Minneapolis, MN : Lerner Publications, [2019] | Series: Searchlight books. cutting-edge stem | Includes bibliographical references and index. | Audience: Ages 8–11. | Audience: Grades 4 to 6.
Identifiers: LCCN 2018006018 (print) | LCCN 2018000273 (ebook) | ISBN 9781541525382 (eb pdf) | ISBN 9781541523456 (lb : alk. paper) | ISBN 9781541527751 (pb : alk. paper)
Subjects: LCSH: Raspberry Pi (Computer)—Juvenile literature. | Pocket computers—Juvenile literature. | Automatic control—Juvenile literature.
Classification: LCC QA76.8.R15 (print) | LCC QA76.8.R15 G63 2019 (ebook) | DDC 004.165—dc23

LC record available at https://lccn.loc.gov/2018006018

Manufactured in the United States of America
1-44418-34677-4/2/2018

Contents

Chapter 1

WHAT IS RASPBERRY PI?

In September 2017, a man in Denmark found a small foam box on the beach. The box was filled with wires, an antenna, a tiny computer, and a camera. It was part of a weather balloon launched two months earlier by students in England.

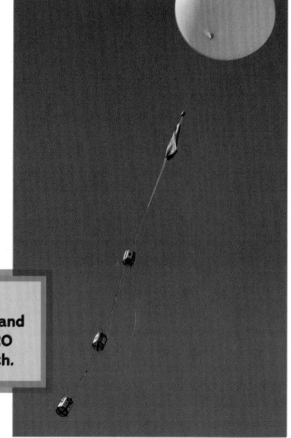

A homemade weather balloon can take pictures and measure temperatures 20 miles (32 km) above Earth.

The green rectangle in this image is a Raspberry Pi. It is connected to a circuit and LED lights.

The weather balloon's tiny computer was a Raspberry Pi. This computer is only the size of a credit card, but it can do just about everything a desktop or laptop computer can do. The other difference between Raspberry Pi and a personal computer is that Raspberry Pi costs only about thirty dollars, and you build it yourself. Since Raspberry Pi first came out in 2012, people around the world have used them to make everything from video games to robots to weather stations.

What's in a Computer?

When you think of a computer, you probably think of something that has a screen and a keyboard. But do you know what's inside a computer that makes it work? A computer uses both hardware and software. Hardware is all the parts of the computer that you can see and touch. Software is the instructions that tell a computer how to complete tasks.

You might use a tablet, a phone, or a laptop every day. All of these devices have hardware and software.

THE MORE MEMORY A COMPUTER HAS, THE MORE QUICKLY AND SMOOTHLY IT WILL RUN.

One of the most important pieces of hardware in a computer is the processor. This is the computer's brain. It follows instructions from the software. Another important part is the RAM, or random access memory. RAM allows the computer to access and store information so it can work quickly. Inside a computer, these parts connect to a thin plate called a circuit board.

This Raspberry Pi is connected to a memory card and several pieces of hardware.

A Raspberry Pi is basically a circuit board. It comes with RAM and a processor. For the computer to work, you also need to connect a power cord, a memory card for long-term storage, and a monitor, keyboard, and mouse to the circuit board. You can even connect your Raspberry Pi to the internet using an Ethernet cable. This hardware can be the same kind that you would use for a regular computer.

The most important computer software is an operating system, which is saved on the memory card. The operating system makes all the hardware work together so that the computer can run. With all of these pieces in place, you can use the Raspberry Pi just like a regular laptop or personal computer.

WITHOUT A MEMORY CARD, A RASPBERRY PI CANNOT START.

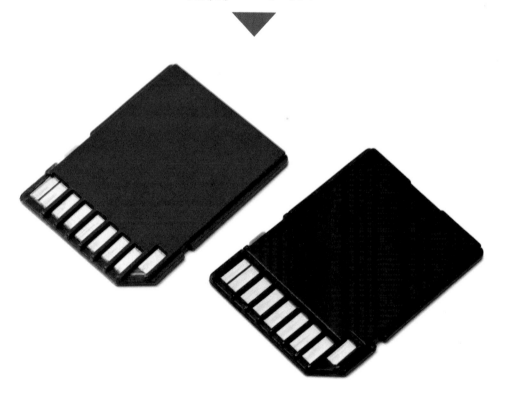

Science Fact or Science Fiction?

You can control your Raspberry Pi with just your voice.

That's a fact! But you'll need a few more pieces of hardware and software to make this work.

You can add a microphone, a speaker, and a program that recognizes your voice to your Raspberry Pi. Once it's all set up, you can ask your Raspberry Pi what time it is. Or you could ask for information about your favorite singer. Your Raspberry Pi will respond with the right answers.

Chapter 2

PROGRAMS AND GAMES

The Raspberry Pi isn't popular just because it is an inexpensive computer. Working with a Raspberry Pi is a great way to learn how computers work. A Raspberry Pi also makes it easy to learn how to write your own computer programs.

Students work with a Raspberry Pi at a summer computer camp.

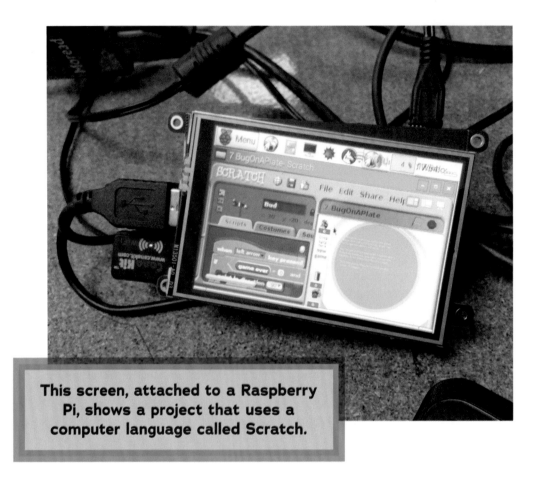

This screen, attached to a Raspberry Pi, shows a project that uses a computer language called Scratch.

Computer programs are instructions written in a special language that computers can understand. There are many different computer languages. Python and Scratch are common languages used for Raspberry Pi. With Raspberry Pi, you can write your own programs for just about anything. You can make your own games and apps, write music, or create an automatic system for watering plants.

Coding Spotlight

Scratch is one of the most popular computer languages to use with Raspberry Pi. It is very simple and easy to learn. Most computer programming languages use lines of words and symbols that can look very complicated. But Scratch uses colorful blocks that fit together. It is easy to see what the instructions mean and how they work together. Scratch is especially useful for creating games and cartoons.

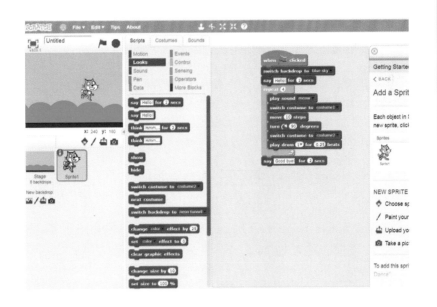

Playing with Pi

Many Raspberry Pi users make and play games with Scratch. One example is a game called Flappy Parrot. Anyone can create a version of this game. With Scratch, you can create a character and a landscape. Then you create obstacles for the character and tell the game how to move the character through the landscape.

SCRATCH BLOCKS TELL THE PARROT HOW TO MOVE BETWEEN THE GREEN PIPES.

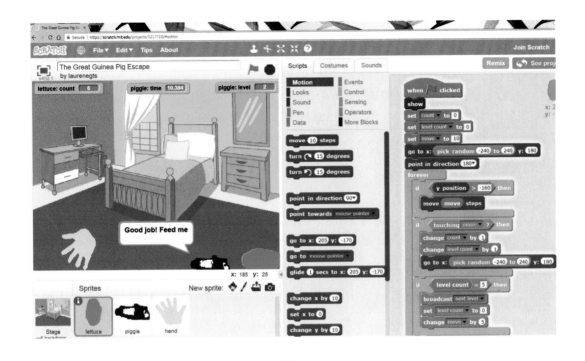

THESE SCRATCH BLOCKS GIVE INSTRUCTIONS FOR MOVING AND FEEDING A GUINEA PIG.

You can use your imagination to create any kind of game! One girl's pet guinea pigs inspired her. She made a game called the Great Guinea Pig Escape. In the game, players get points when the guinea pigs eat lettuce.

Using a Raspberry Pi, you can download and play other computer games too. There is even a special version of *Minecraft* just for Raspberry Pi. You can play the game as you would on any other computer, or you can use a programming language to write new instructions. You can change how the game looks and how you play it!

These students work on a *Minecraft* scene using a Raspberry Pi.

Chapter 3

SHARING IDEAS

Once you know how the Raspberry Pi works and how to write a program, you can do all kinds of cool projects. Many people who work with Raspberry Pi share their ideas and their finished projects on the Raspberry Pi website. This way, others can try the projects or give ideas about how to make them better. One woman shared a system she created to check on her dog when she isn't home. And someone known as the Raspberry Pi Guy made an electric skateboard.

Raspberry Pi Guy's skateboard is controlled by a Nintendo Wii remote and can go up to 18 miles (30 km) per hour.

Students work on projects at a meetup event called a Raspberry Jam.

The Raspberry Pi organization holds events called Raspberry Jams where people who love Raspberry Pi can meet. They learn more about Raspberry Pi and share their projects and ideas. The organization also has coding clubs, websites, magazines, and books to teach people about computers and coding.

More Hardware

Many Raspberry Pi projects require extra hardware or brand-new software. For example, the woman who made the system to check on her dog added speakers and a microphone. This way, she can hear when the dog barks. She said that to make the project even better, she could add a camera or other sensors. And the Raspberry Pi Guy wrote about one hundred lines of instructions in Python to control his skateboard.

THIS RASPBERRY PI IS CONNECTED TO A SPEAKER.

Say you want to make a motion detector for your room. You want the device to turn on a light automatically when someone comes in. You would need some extra hardware and a new program. You would connect lights to the computer as well as a sensor that recognizes when a person walks by. Your program would tell the computer to turn on the light when the sensor detected a person coming into the room.

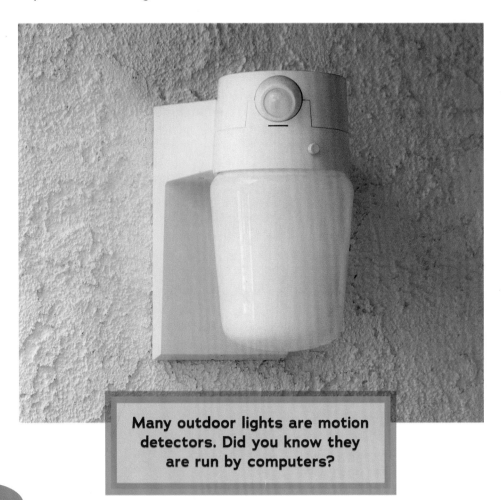

Many outdoor lights are motion detectors. Did you know they are run by computers?

Science Fact or Science Fiction?

A Raspberry Pi can stop criminals.

That's true!

Some locks open by scanning a fingerprint. Everybody has different fingerprints, so it seems safe. But some people have figured out how to make fake fingerprints to break into these locks. So three college professors used a Raspberry Pi to make a better fingerprint reader. They called it RaspiReader. Their invention was easy to make. It uses a light and two cameras, and it can even spot fake fingerprints.

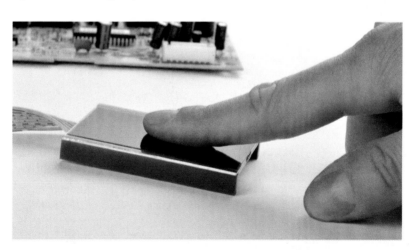

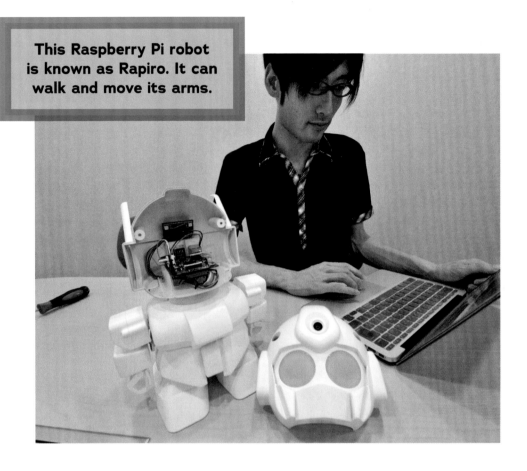

This Raspberry Pi robot is known as Rapiro. It can walk and move its arms.

Another popular Raspberry Pi project is building remote-controlled robots. One man programmed his robot to pick up Ping-Pong balls from the floor. A big fork on the front of the robot scooped up the balls. A cage on the robot held them. A camera on the robot's head allowed the person controlling the robot to see where the balls were and to move the robot in the right way to pick them up.

Chapter 4

ENDLESS POSSIBILITIES

Many people enjoy trying out new ideas with Raspberry Pi just for fun. They like to write new programs and add new hardware to see what works. Other people see problems in the world and want to use Raspberry Pi to fix them.

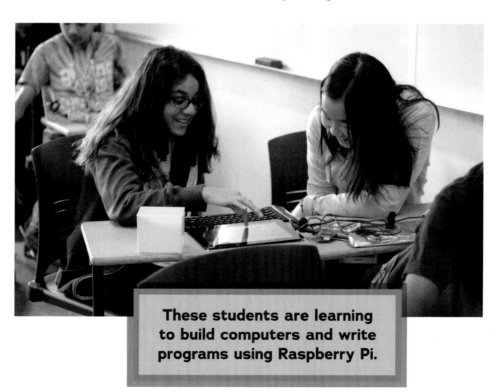

These students are learning to build computers and write programs using Raspberry Pi.

Scientists used a Raspberry Pi to study the Okavango Delta, a large swampy area in Botswana.

One team of scientists went on an expedition to Botswana. They traveled through the southern African country by canoe. With a Raspberry Pi and a network of sensors, they collected information about the air and water. The Raspberry Pi was easy to carry in the canoes. The scientists could gather information quickly and easily. Then they shared it with people right away using a website.

Learning with Raspberry Pi

In some regions of the world, students have never used a computer. Some schools cannot afford to buy computers. But because Raspberry Pi is so inexpensive, schools without much money can buy them.

Some schools have lots of computers and other technology. But many schools around the world cannot afford to buy these tools for students.

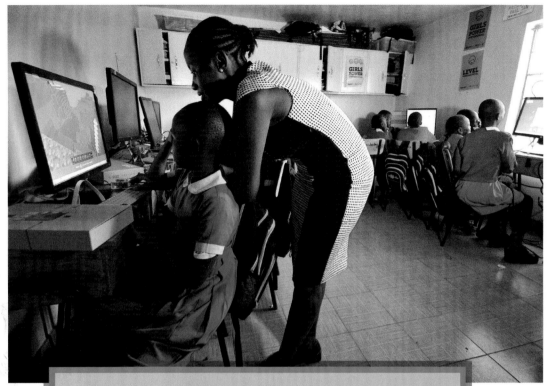

A teacher at a school in Nairobi, Kenya, shows students how to use Raspberry Pi computers. The school provides free education in an area where many people cannot afford to go to school.

A man named Dominique Laloux raised money to buy twenty-one Raspberry Pi computers for a school in Togo, West Africa. The school built a complete computer lab, and students are programming to learn and for fun! Laloux hopes to continue raising money to help other schools build computer labs too.

Kids can also find ways to use Raspberry Pi to help others. Hari Bhimaraju, a twelve-year-old girl in Cupertino, California, created a tool to help visually impaired people learn chemistry. Hari's creation used sound and lights. It cost very little to make. She presented her creation at the White House Science Fair in 2016. She even shook then president Barack Obama's hand!

Hari's tool won a first place award in the Synopsys Silicon Valley Science and Technology Championship.

Raspberry Pi in Action

Students at a school in England used a Raspberry Pi to create a weather station. They connected sensors to the Raspberry Pi to measure air pressure, wind speed, temperature, and other weather factors. The students shared local weather information with schools around the world on the Raspberry Pi website. In North Carolina, students created a weather station to track the solar eclipse in August 2017. They found that the temperature dropped during the eclipse.

Pi for the future

Raspberry Pi is a source of fun and creativity, and it's an important tool for learning. Computers are part of everyday life. Understanding how they work and knowing how to write programs will become even more important in the future. What will you create with Raspberry Pi?

STUDENTS WORK ON RASPBERRY PI PROJECTS AT A RASPBERRY JAM IN ENGLAND.

▼

Glossary

app: a computer program that performs a special function

download: to save information from the internet onto a computer

expedition: a trip taken to learn or discover something

monitor: a screen that displays images

motion detector: a device that senses when something is moving

program: a set of instructions that tells a computer what to do

sensor: a device that responds to heat, light, sound, or movement

visually impaired: unable to see well

Learn More about Raspberry Pi

Books

Harris, Patricia. *Understanding Coding with Raspberry Pi*. New York: PowerKids, 2016. Learn more about writing computer programs, and find out about the history of Raspberry Pi.

Severance, Charles R., and Kristin Fontichiaro. *Raspberry Pi*. Ann Arbor, MI: Cherry Lake, 2014. Find out how to set up and begin using your own Raspberry Pi.

Wood, Kevin. *Create Computer Games with Scratch*. Minneapolis: Lerner Publications, 2018. Follow the instructions to create your own computer game.

Websites

Raspberry Pi
https://www.raspberrypi.org
Learn more about Raspberry Pi, and find projects, news, or Raspberry Jams and coding clubs near you.

Raspberry Pi Projects
https://www.kidscodecs.com/raspberry-pi-projects/
This site includes videos and links to more information about setting up your Raspberry Pi, playing *Minecraft*, and making cool projects.

Scratch
https://scratch.mit.edu/
Find games, projects, stories, and tips from other Scratch users on the Scratch website.

Index

Photo Acknowledgments

Image credits: Eclipse Ballooning Project 2017/Montana State University, p. 4; goodcat/ Shutterstock.com, p. 5; Uber Images/Shutterstock.com, p. 6; Nor Gal/Shutterstock.com, p. 7; JoeFox Liverpool/Radharc Images/Alamy Stock Photo, p. 8; IB Photography/Shutterstock. com, p. 9; True Images/Alamy Stock Photo, p. 10; Kevin Jarrett/Flickr (CC by 2.0), pp. 11, 12, 16; Screengrab of Scratch. Scratch is a project of the Lifelong Kindergarten Group at the MIT Media Lab, p. 13; Screengrab of Flappy Parrot by PaulSinnett on Scratch, p. 14; Screengrab of the Great Guinea Pig Escape by Lauren Egts on Scratch, p. 15; Matthew "Raspberry Pi Guy" Timmons-Brown, p. 17; MadLab Manchester Digital Laboratory/Flickr (CC BY-SA 2.0), p. 18; Gareth Halfacree/Flickr (CC BY-SA 2.0), p. 19; Dancestrokes/Shutterstock.com, p. 20; s-cphoto/Getty Images, p. 21; Yoshikazu Tsuno/AFP/Getty Images, p. 22; Stephen Chin/Flickr (CC BY 2.0), p. 23; Kelly Cheng Travel Photography/Moment/Getty Images, p. 24; Air Images/ Shutterstock.com, p. 25; Simon Maina/AFP/Getty Images, p. 26; Gayatri Bhimaraju/Wikimedia Commons (CC BY-SA 4.0), p. 27; CrimeScene/Shutterstock.com, p. 28; Jeff Gilbert/Alamy Stock Photo, p. 29.

Cover: Emma Gibbs/Moment/Getty Images.